TOWNSHIP OF WAS

P9-DEV-437

3 9149 09107214 0

TOWNSHIP OF WASHINGTON PUBLIC LIBRARY
144 WOODFIELD ROAD
TOWNSHIP OF WASHINGTON, N.J. 07676

For my daughter, Beth-Alison Berggren,
and in memory of my son, Peter Dane Bauer
M. D. B.

To my son, Kai Holmes,
the Magician
E. H.

With gratitude for my blessings, editor Liz Bicknell
and agent Rubin Pfeffer   M. D. B.

Text copyright © 2018 by Marion Dane Bauer
Illustrations copyright © 2018 by Ekua Holmes

All rights reserved. No part of this book may be reproduced, transmitted,
or stored in an information retrieval system in any form or by any means, graphic,
electronic, or mechanical, including photocopying, taping, and recording,
without prior written permission from the publisher.

First edition 2018

Library of Congress Catalog Card Number pending
ISBN 978-0-7636-7883-8

18 19 20 21 22 23 TLF 10 9 8 7 6 5 4 3 2 1

Printed in Dongguan, Guangdong, China

This book was typeset in Caudex.
The illustrations were done with hand-marbled paper and collage
and assembled digitally.

Candlewick Press
99 Dover Street
Somerville, Massachusetts 02144

visit us at www.candlewick.com

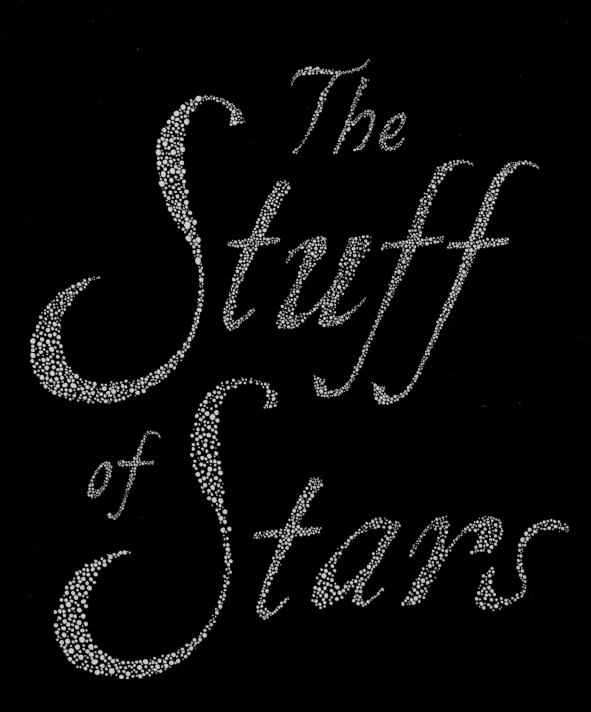

The Stuff of Stars

Marion Dane Bauer
illustrated by Ekua Holmes

CANDLEWICK PRESS

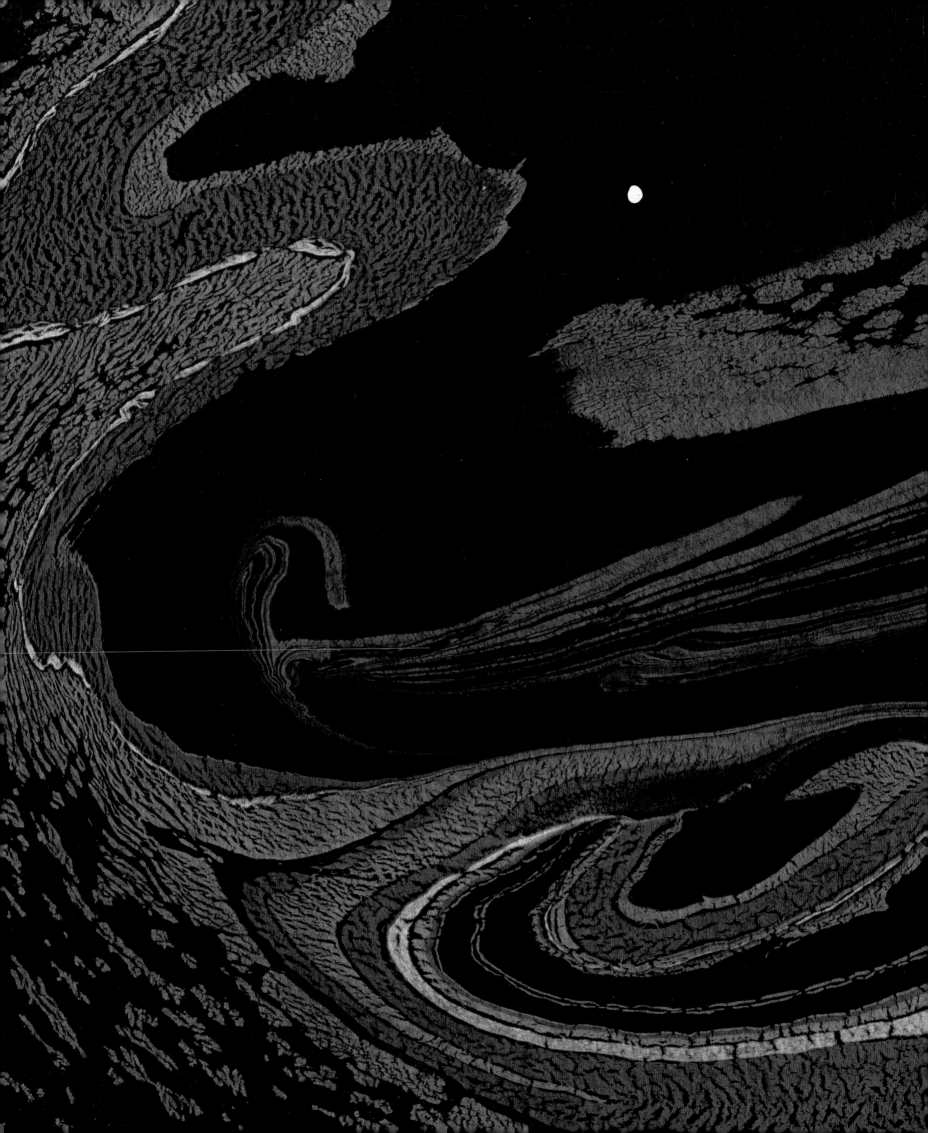

In the dark,

in the dark,

in the deep, deep dark,

a speck floated,

invisible as thought,

weighty as God.

There was yet no time,

there was yet no space.

No up,

no down,

no edge,

no center.

No Earth with soaring hawks,

scuttling beetles,

trees reaching for the sky.

There was no sky.

No you.

No me.

Only the speck,

waiting,

waiting . . .

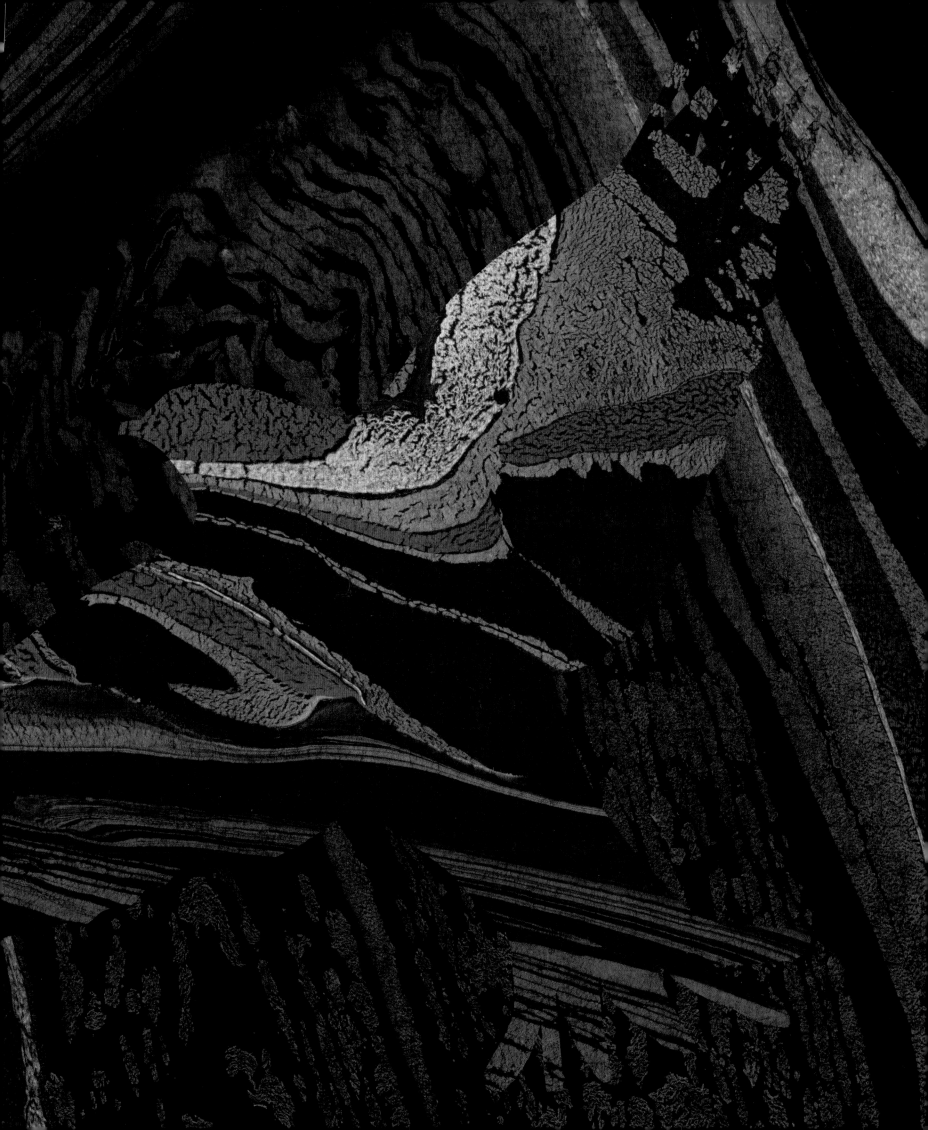

And then

the beginning

of the beginning

of all beginnings

went

BANG!

And in a trillionth
of a second . . .
our universe was born.
A cloud of gas
unfolded,
unfurled,
zigged,
zagged,

stretched,

collided,

expanded . . .

expanded . . .

expanded . . .

Bits bumped,

gathered,

fused.

And throughout the cosmos
stars caught fire.
Trillions of stars,
but still no planets
to attend those stars.   then no oceans,
And if no planets,

no mountains,

no hippopotami.

No violets blooming
in a shady wood,
no crickets singing
to the night.
No day,
no night.

The stars burned and burned.

They burned so long

and so hot

that some of them

EXPLODED,

flinging stardust everywhere.

And the ash of those dying stars

gathered into planets,

and the planets

circled other stars.

But still . . .

no bluebirds,

no butterflies,

still no snails,

no giraffes,

still no you,

no me.

The planets closest to their star
stayed very hot.
The ones far away
grew very cold.

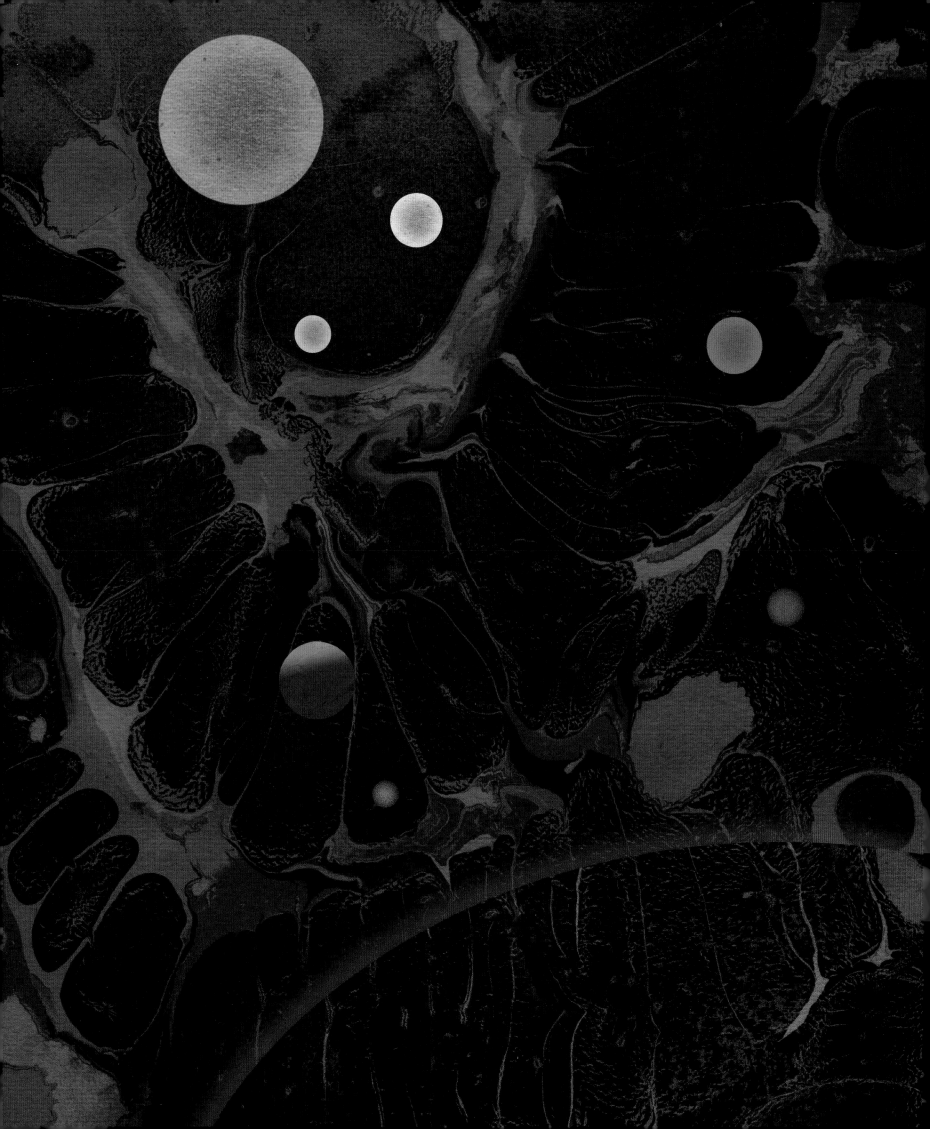

But one lucky planet,

a fragile blue ball we call Earth,

was neither too far

nor too near.

It circled its yellow star,

the one we call the Sun,

from just the right distance

and with just the right tilt

to be sometimes warm,

sometimes cool.

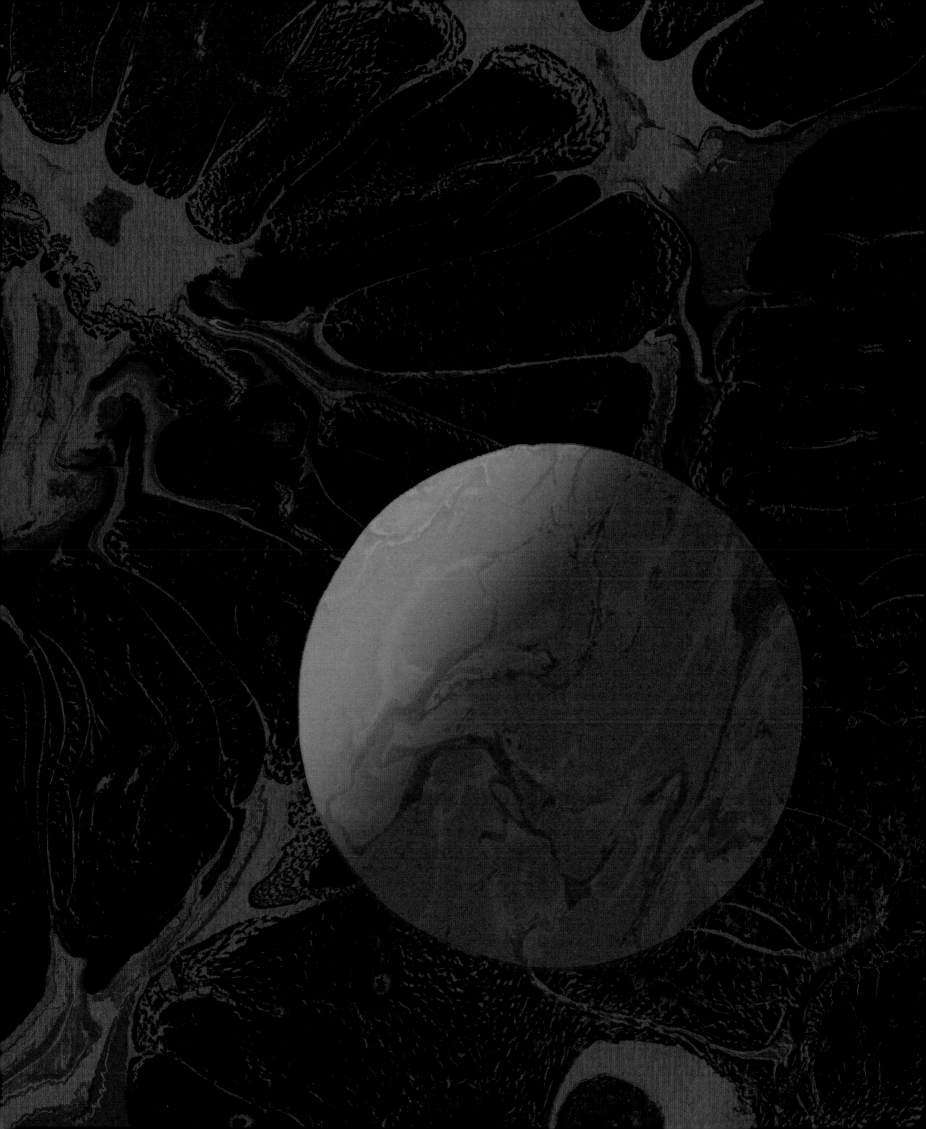

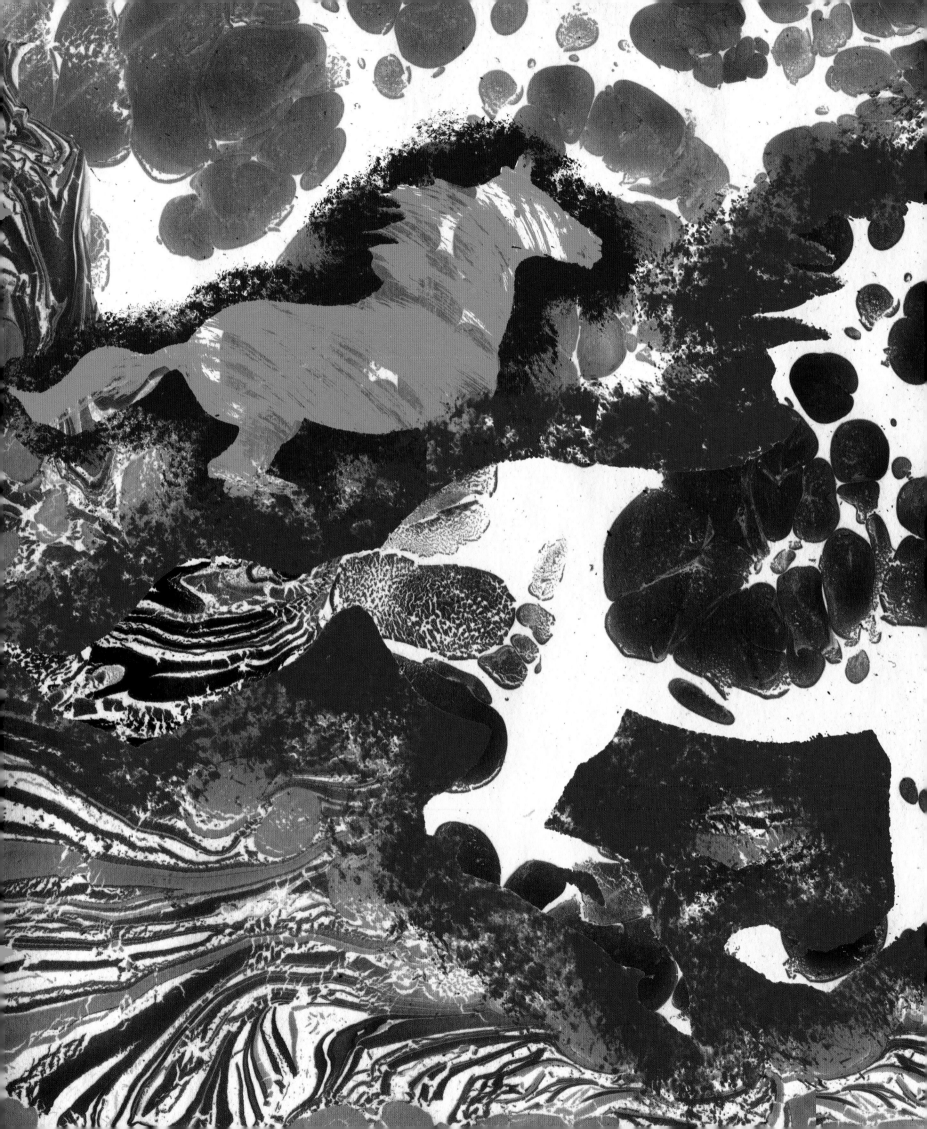

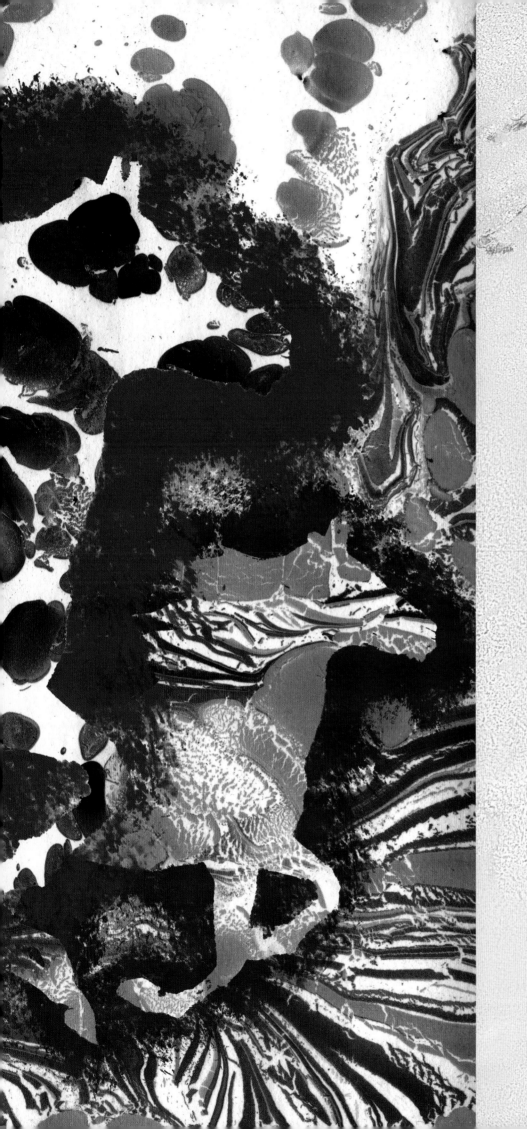

Perfect for turning

that starry stuff

into mitochondria,

jellyfish,

spiders,

into ferns

and sharks,

into daisies

and galloping horses.

Again and again

stardust

gave birth

to stardust.

Dinosaurs lived and died,

making room for humans.

Our great-great-great grandparents

and all before them

lived and died,

making room for more

and more children.

Then one day . . .

in the dark,

in the dark,

in the deep, deep dark,

another speck floated,

invisible as dreams,

special as Love.

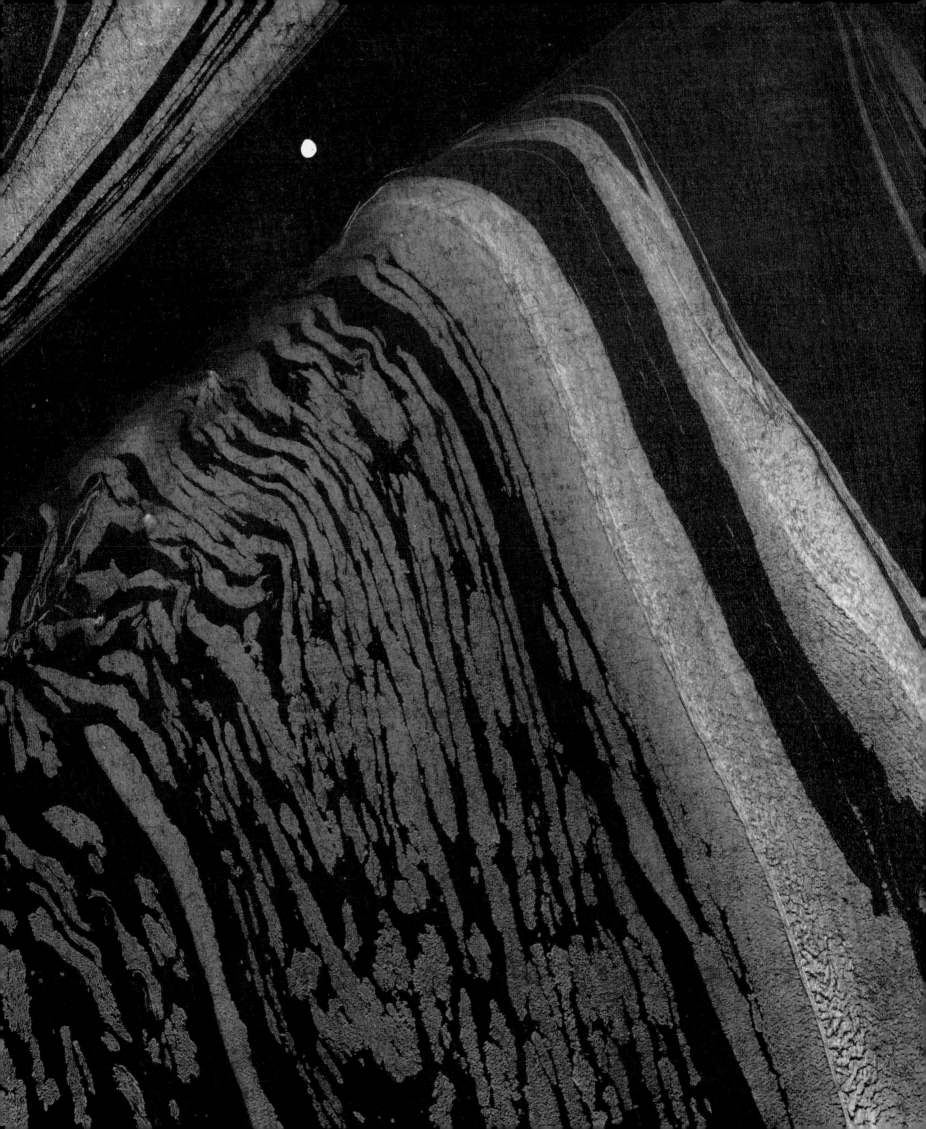

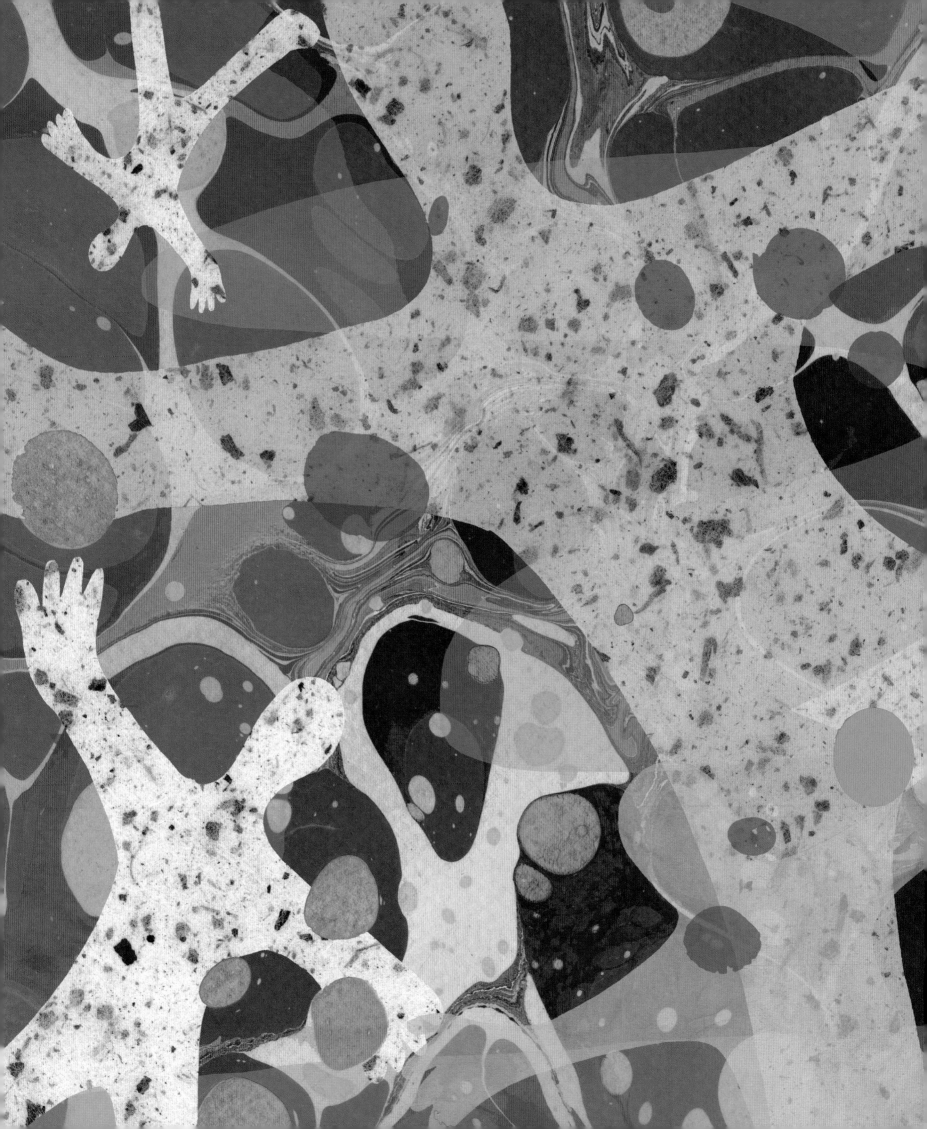

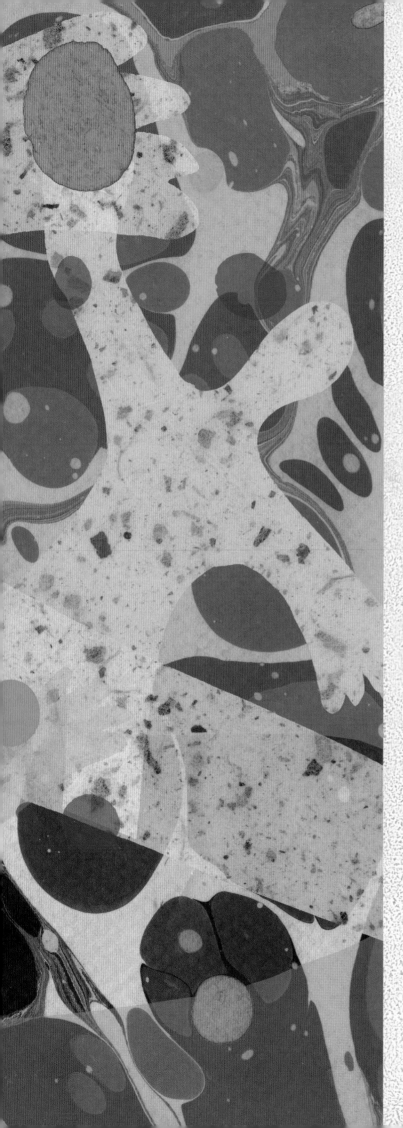

Waiting,

waiting,

dividing,

changing,

growing.

Until at last,

YOU burst into the world.

You took a big breath

of the same air

once breathed

by woolly mammoths.

You cried tears

that were once salty seas.

Your hair

once the carbon in a leaf.

You
and the velvet moss,
the caterpillars,
the lions.

You
and the singing whales,
the larks,
the frogs.

You,

and me

loving you.

All of us

the stuff of stars.

FEB 1 4 2013